MR NIBBLE CALLS A DOCTOR

JANE PILGRIM

Illustrated by F. Stocks May

HODDER AND STOUGHTON

LONDON SYDNEY AUCKLAND TORONTO

Down in the Big Wood Mr Nibble and his three little bunnies, Rosy, Posy and Christopher, had gone to collect wood. Mr Nibble had his big axe and the three little bunnies had their baskets.

Chop, chop, chop went the axe.
And the little bunnies neatly
packed the wood in their baskets.

Then with a crash an old rotten branch fell right on top of Mr Nibble—and there he lay pinned to the ground, unable to move even a whisker!

In vain Rosy, Posy and Christopher tried to free him. Poor Mr Nibble groaned aloud. He was very frightened and his leg hurt him very much. He thought he would never be able to move again.

Then he saw Joe Robin hopping cheerfully through the bushes and he called loudly to him: 'Help! Help! Joe Robin, fetch me a doctor! Fetch Ernest Owl! Find somebody strong to rescue me!' Joe Robin was very surprised and very upset, and flew off as fast as he could to tell Ernest Owl what had happened.

Ernest Owl was getting his dinner ready when Joe Robin flew in with the call for help. 'Come quickly, please—there has been an accident. Mr Nibble needs a doctor!'

'I will come at once,' said Ernest Owl. 'But we must have more help. Fetch Marcus Mouse and George the Kitten and tell them to bring a rope. And ask Lucy Mouse to hurry to Mrs Nibble and help her get ready for the arrival of an accident—hot-water bottles, strong tea and bandages!' And off they flew—Joe Robin for more help and Ernest Owl to the rescue.

Mr Nibble was glad and comforted to see Ernest Owl. 'My friend, I will save you,' said Ernest Owl, and he told the little bunnies to rest from pushing the branch while he studied the situation and made a plan.

Soon Joe Robin arrived with George the Kitten and Marcus Mouse and a big rope. They tied the rope firmly round the branch and when Ernest Owl cried: 'One, two, three, go!' they pulled their hardest, and the little bunnies pushed their hardest, and Ernest Owl held on to Mr Nibble. But they could not move the branch.

Then Ernest Owl thought of Mrs Squirrel and Hazel, who were sure to be somewhere in the wood. And he hooted loudly: 'Help! Help! We need help!' And very soon the two squirrels came springing over the branches. 'Come and pull!' ordered Ernest Owl. 'Come and help rescue Mr Nibble!'

So they all pulled and pushed their hardest, and suddenly Mr Nibble was freed.

But although Mr Nibble no longer had the branch on top of him, he still could not get up. 'My leg hurts so much,' he told Ernest Owl. And Ernest Owl, who had once read a book called *How to be a Good Doctor*, felt him carefully all over and said: 'I'm afraid, Mr Nibble, that you have broken your leg.'

Very quickly Ernest Owl found a strong, straight stick. Marcus Mouse took two large clean hankies out of his pocket. Then Mr Nibble's leg was bound up, and they carried him gently home.

Mrs Nibble and Lucy Mouse were waiting anxiously, and how glad they were to tuck up Mr Nibble safely in bed and watch him happily drink a large cup of strong, sweet tea!

In a few days he was up on crutches, and the first thing that he and Mrs Nibble did was to walk down to thank Ernest Owl for being such a good doctor.
'I am glad I have been of use,' said Ernest. 'I like to do all I can for everyone at Blackberry Farm.'

BLACKBERRY FARM BOOKS

Emily The Goat
Rusty The Sheepdog
Postman Joe
Mrs Nibble
Mother Hen and Mary
Naughty George
Mrs Squirrel and Hazel
Ernest Owl Starts a School
The Adventures of Walter
Lucy Mouse Keeps a Secret
Walter Duck and Winifred
Mrs Nibble Moves House
Christmas at Blackberry Farm
Little Martha
A Bunny in Trouble
Hide and Seek at Blackberry Farm
Poor Mr Nibble
Snow at Blackberry Farm
Mr Nibble Calls a Doctor
Sam Sparrow
Saturday at Blackberry Farm
Mr Mole Takes Charge
Sports Day at Blackberry Farm
Henry Goes Visiting
The Birthday Picnic